NIGHT OF THE CHUPACABRA

GRAVESIDE READS VOL. 2
BOOK 1

D.L. WINCHESTER

GRAVESIDE READS

For Atlas

NIGHT OF THE CHUPACABRA

1

The jeep bounced across the desert, following a narrow path through the mesquite and scrub.

"Carlos, slow down!" Abbi shrieked, as a branch slapped the windshield on her side.

Carlos, a tan young man with a bright smile, turned the radio up. "I can't hear you!"

Abbi rolled her brown eyes. Pushing her blonde hair out of her face, she leaned across the center console to yell in his ear. "Slow down!"

He shook his head, but moved his foot to the brake pedal.

"Thank you." Abbi flashed him a smile as she settled back into her seat.

"About time," Dani, Abbi's sister, said from the back seat.

Carlos shook his head. "You're nowhere near as fun as your sister."

"Someone's got to be responsible," Dani snapped back. "Besides, y'all invited me."

Carlos jerked his head toward the backseat. "Reece didn't

1

want to be a third wheel, and Abbi thought you two would get along. I can already tell you have a lot in common."

Dani ignored the sarcasm and looked at Reece, sitting behind Carlos. He had barely spoken all day, and now, seeing her looking at him, he turned away and blushed.

Dani sighed. Off-roading in the Big Bend of Texas wasn't her usual idea of fun, but when Abbi had asked her to come, she'd jumped at the chance, hoping it meant things between them were improving. Instead, it looked like she'd been invited to keep this nerd distracted while Carlos and Abbi...

The jeep skidded to a halt, snapping Dani back to the moment.

"Why'd we stop?" Reece asked.

"Look over there." Carlos pointed out the window to a fenced area off the path. A metal arch stood over the gate, a cross welded to the top. "I think it's an old cemetery."

"What?" Abbi leaned across him, and Dani saw Carlos cop a feel.

"That's gotta be really old," Reece said. "We're thirty miles from the nearest pavement. There must have been a settlement here, and now this cemetery is all that's left."

"And that's why we brought you, Reece," Carlos said. "You know all the shit no one else cares about."

Reece blushed, and Dani felt a moment of sympathy for him. "I think it's interesting."

"See?" Carlos said, opening the door. "A match made in heaven. Or hell, depending on how interesting you think Reece is."

"Where are you going?" Abbi asked.

"To check out the cemetery. It looks cool."

Abbi grinned, and opened her door too. "It's spooky. Especially with Halloween coming up next month."

Dani climbed out behind her. "It is pretty cool," she admitted.

The cemetery was overgrown, with mesquite bushes growing between the graves, each one piled high with dirt and rocks and marked with weathered wooden crosses. Toward the back, a few tombstones were visible.

"Watch for rattlesnakes," Reece said as Carlos opened the gate. "If you get bit, it's a long way to the hospital."

Dani shivered in the heat. "I hate snakes."

Reece carefully put an arm around her. "I'll keep an eye out for you."

Dani rolled out of his grasp. "What the hell are you going to do, hit them with a calculator?"

Reece looked like he'd been hit, and adjusted his glasses before looking to Carlos or Abbi for support.

Figures, Dani thought. She didn't know how Carlos had ended up friends with someone like Reece. Reece was the kind of person who excelled in the classroom, but had no clue how to act in the real world. A sophomore like Carlos and Abbi, she knew they were in some classes together, but hadn't realized they were close enough to hang out. Out of all the kids at their university, the eagle scout was the last one she expected Carlos and Abbi to hang out with.

Lord, he probably was an eagle scout, she thought, watching him study the graves. Carlos and Abbi had moved toward the back of the cemetery, hidden by the mesquite.

"This guy died in 1898!" Abbi called.

"1913 here," Carlos replied.

Reece moved closer to Dani. "Are you okay?"

She shrugged. "This isn't really my thing, you know. I'd rather be back in my dorm than out here with those two." She jerked her head toward Carlos and Abbi.

He smiled. "I'm a little out of my comfort zone here too." She noticed his blue eyes behind his glasses. Without the glasses, Reece wouldn't be bad looking, she thought.

"Hey! Look at this!" Abbi called. Reece and Dani moved through the scrub to join her.

Carlos had already reached her, wrapping his arm around her waist. "Looks like an old mine shaft."

A hole had been dug out of the hillside beyond the cemetery, supported by weathered timbers.

"I wonder what's down there?" Abbi said. "Gold? Silver?"

"An accident waiting to happen," Dani muttered. Her sister could be a little too adventurous sometimes.

Carlos slid his hand down and squeezed Abbi's ass. "I love finding things to explore."

Abbi laughed, and Dani rolled her eyes. Reece looked at her, then sighed. "I wish I was that bold."

Dani gave him a smile. "Be glad you aren't. Not every girl likes a guy like Carlos."

A pause. "Really?"

"Yeah. He's kind of annoying."

Reece laughed. "I don't spend a ton of time around girls. I'm never sure how to act or what to say."

Jesus. "We don't bite," Dani said.

"Speak for yourself!" Abbi called, earning an eye roll.

"You're in Econ 2 with Professor Ertz, right?" Dani asked.

He nodded.

"You think she pops the baby out before finals?"

Reece shook his head. "I bet it shows up during our exam."

"Jesus!" Dani laughed. "I'd throw up."

He grinned. "Me too. I'm...not a fan of blood."

"Aww, do you two need to get a room?" Carlos called, turning toward them.

Dani flipped him off.

"I think your sister would have something to say if I took your invitation," Carlos grinned.

Abbi grabbed his hand. "You're mine, baby."

"Let's get back to campus," Carlos suggested. "We can drop these two off and find a place to do that exploring I mentioned."

2

As they walked back to the jeep, Abbi and Carlos in the lead, Reece stopped Dani.

"Uh, so I know I haven't been the best company today," he said, scratching at the back of his head. "But I was wondering if you'd give me another chance, and we could hang out sometime?"

Dani smiled. He was growing on her, his awkwardness becoming appealing. And he was cute, especially if she could get him to wear contacts.

"I think we can do that."

He breathed a sigh of relief. "Thanks."

"Y'all coming?" Carlos called from the jeep. "Andale! Andale!"

Reece shook his head, and they walked over and got in the backseat.

Dating him would get Abbi off my back, Dani thought. *And he doesn't seem like the type to pressure me to do things I don't want to.* Dani was proud her virginity was going to survive her freshman year of college.

Abbi's didn't survive her freshman year of high school!

Jealousy! Her mind warned her. She'd spent a lot of time in therapy talking about how her older sister seemed to get everything first. Boobs. Butt. Boyfriends. Meanwhile, by the time Dani blossomed, she had a reputation for having a stick up her ass, and no one was interested in her. College was supposed to have been a fresh start, but the ghosts of high school still haunted her.

Until today.

"Um."

Dani looked down and realized her hand was on top of Reece's. She looked up at him, and realized he didn't know what to do.

She squeezed his hand. "Sorry. It just felt natural."

"It's okay. I like it."

For a moment, they looked at each other.

Kiss him! her brain demanded.

It's too damn soon!

Who gives a fuck?

"Uh, folks," Carlos said from the front seat, snapping her attention back to the moment. "We've got a problem." He twisted the key in the ignition, but instead of the engine roaring to life, all they heard was *click-click-click-click.*

"That clicking is the starter," Reece said. "Since it's working, it's probably a dead battery. Maybe the alternator."

"We can just jump it, right?" Abbi asked.

"On what?" Carlos asked.

"Oh, right."

"There's no cell service, and we're thirty miles from the nearest paved road." Carlos looked at his watch. "Sunset's in about three hours, so it'll probably be tomorrow before they find us."

"Sounds like an adventure," Abbi said.

Carlos grinned. "Maybe with some exploring?"

"That could be fun."

Reece pulled his hand out and put it on top of Dani's. "Don't worry. I packed an emergency kit. I've got everything we need."

She smiled at him. He was the type to come prepared. She'd planned ahead some, bringing a couple quarts of water, some snacks, and a flashlight, but Reece probably had an entire camping section in his backpack.

"The border patrol will probably find us," he continued. "They're always doing patrols out here. And if they don't, my parents know what we're doing, and they'll come looking if we're out too long."

"How will they know where to look?"

Reece pulled a necklace out from under his shirt and held up the pendant. "There's a GPS chip embedded in this."

"Seriously?"

He shrugged. "They're worried someone might kidnap me for ransom."

"Sounds kind of weird."

"It's something they have to keep in mind," Reece said. "They've got enough money to buy our college at least twice."

Dani felt her mouth drop open.

Kinda cute AND rich?

I might just have to thank Abbi when we get out of this!

Baaaaaaaaaaaaat!

They looked up to see a goat standing in the middle of the road.

"What the fuck?" Carlos asked.

"It's a goat," Reece said, leaning between the seats for a closer look.

"No shit, man. I know what a fucking goat is. I just didn't expect to see one all the way out here!"

"Some kind of wild goat?" Abbi asked.

"They probably had goats out here when the mine was open," Reece speculated. "This could be a descendant."

The goat was brown, with long horns curving off its skull, yellow eyes staring into the jeep.

Baaaaaaaaaaaaaaaaaat.

It turned and disappeared into the brush beside the road.

"Well, that was freaky," Abbi said.

Carlos shook his head. "Fucking goat."

3

"I'm hungry," Abbi said.

"I didn't bring anything to eat," Carlos replied. "I wasn't planning on being stuck out here."

Dani looked at Reece and shook her head. Reaching into her backpack, she took out a pack of peanut butter crackers and handed them to her sister.

"Thanks," Abbi said, tearing them open.

The sun was sinking lower in the west. Reece had his backpack out and was examining the contents.

"You good?" Dani asked.

He nodded. "Just doing a quick inventory, figuring out how to ration things." Reece jerked his head toward the front seat. "Sounds like they don't have anything to contribute."

Dani shook her head. "Nah. They're lucky they brought us." She handed him her backpack. "I didn't plan to share, but I'll put what I brought in the pot too."

Reece smiled. "Anything helps."

Baaaaaaaaat.

Dani laughed. "We may have to ration for another."

Reece shook his head. "The goat can find its own food."

"Goats," Carlos said from the front seat.

"What?" Reece and Dani looked out the windshield.

There was a herd of goats in the road in front of the jeep. Some were grazing on the bushes lining the road, while others just stared at the jeep.

"They're kinda cute," Dani said.

"They're kinda spooky," Carlos said, slumping down in his seat. "I wish they'd get out of here. It's hard enough being stuck without a fucking audience."

Reece was digging in his backpack, ignoring Carlos. He pulled out a couple of packets, along with a strange looking gizmo and a small pot.

"What's that?" Dani asked.

"A camp stove," he said. "I'm gonna make us some supper."

Carlos whipped around. "Did you say supper?"

Reece nodded. "It won't be a feast, but it'll be something."

Abbi shook her head. "What are you, some kind of boy scout?"

"Eagle scout," Reece replied.

"Nerd," Carlos teased, but he smiled when he said it.

"No dessert for you," Reece joked.

As the sun sank over the western horizon, the four of them sat around a small fire near the cemetery gate, keeping warm, the remains of their meal in the pot on the burner.

"That was good," Dani said.

"It sure was," Abbi added.

Dani put her hand on Reece's knee. "Thanks, Eagle Scout."

He blushed, then stood up quickly. "I've gotta go get us some more wood."

Carlos waited until Reece was out of sight to grin. "I think he busted a nut when you touched him."

"Shut up, Carlos," Abbi said.

"It's not like you brought anything to contribute," Dani added.

He shrugged. "So we get to have a little campout. I didn't figure that would make you two fall in love with him."

"I'm just being appreciative," Abbi said, getting to her feet and stretching. "There's only one man out here I want, and he ain't gathering firewood."

Carlos got up too. "Now that's what I like to hear."

Dani rolled her eyes. "Y'all need to get a room."

"How about a cemetery?" Carlos asked.

"Spooky," Abbi said, turning to look at the gate.

"You wanna?" Carlos asked.

"We'll have to be quiet," Abbi said. "I wouldn't want to offend the sensibilities of certain people." She shot a glance at Dani, who shook her head.

"It wouldn't be the first time I heard you."

"Come on," Carlos said, taking her hand. "We can be plenty quiet."

They'd barely disappeared into the brush beyond the gate when Reece returned, his arms full of mesquite branches. "Where'd they go?"

"To fuck," Dani said, taking a sip of her water and watching Reece out of the corner of her eye. His face turned bright red, just as she'd figured it would. "You've never done that, I take it."

He shook his head. "I was an altar boy. That's not the kind of thing I was supposed to think about." He paused, and Dani realized he wanted to say more.

"Why do I think the altar boy has a wild side?"

Another pause. "Because ever since I saw you, I've wanted...to do that."

This time, Dani blushed. "Me?"

He shrugged. "There's not much sense in denying I've got a crush on you. Hell, you probably already figured that out. When I heard Carlos talking about coming riding out here with Abbi, I offered them a thousand dollars each if they'd bring me and talk you into coming."

"A thousand?" Dani's jaw dropped. "You paid two thousand bucks for a chance to get in my pants?"

His eyes went wide, and he put out his hands. "No! It's not like that, I promise. I just wanted to spend time with you to see if you were as wonderful as I thought. In case you didn't notice, I'm kind of socially awkward. I knew I'd never have the nerve to ask you out, or even to just hang out. But this way..." He shrugged. "It worked for me, so I ran with it."

Reece turned away from her, positioning sticks on the fire, obviously avoiding Dani's gaze.

She took a deep breath. "It feels weird. Like, is it really worth two thousand bucks just to hang out with me?"

"I'd've paid more," Reece said. "I thought about offering to pay you, but I didn't want you to just like me for my money."

Dani knelt next to him. "Hey, I'm human, just like you. If you want to spend time with me, all you have to do is ask, not open your wallet. I put on my pants the same way you do."

"I'd like to see you take them off."

He said it so fast, Dani almost didn't catch it. When she looked at him, he was the reddest she'd ever seen him.

"Reece, you dog," she whispered, grinning.

"I'm sorry," he stammered. "I don't know what came over me."

"No, I like this side of you. The eagle scout's coming out of his shell."

"You don't...you can smack me or shun me, whatever happens when people say things like that."

"How about this?" She took his hand and pulled him to his

feet." Stepping closer, she put it on her ass before leaning in and kissing him.

For a moment, he was too shocked to do anything. Then he kissed back. His inexperience showed—the kiss was wet and sloppy, almost like he was trying to eat her lips, but it still felt right. After a moment, he seemed to remember where his hand was, and tried to move it away and squeeze at the same time.

"Relax," Dani whispered, breaking the kiss for a moment. "I wouldn't have put it there if I didn't want it there."

What had gotten into her? Was this his money talking, her wanting him to have something to show for his two thousand bucks? No, she realized. She wanted this too, to be swept off her feet by a genuinely good guy, even if his methods were kind of unconventional.

Reece nodded, then they were kissing again. This time, he squeezed her ass, and she responded by sliding her hand under his shirt. He jumped a little, but settled in. By the time they broke apart for the second time, he was getting the hang of kissing.

Even if he wasn't, Dani had already decided to kiss him again.

"Wow," he gasped.

Dani smiled. "You like that?"

He nodded, his arms around her, holding her in an embrace.

"So what are you thinking?" she asked.

Reece froze, drawing a chuckle.

"Out with it. Come on," she said.

"If that's what I get for suggesting you take off your pants, I wonder what would happen if I asked you to take your shirt off." He turned red, but was grinning at the same time.

Dani leaned in and whispered, "Maybe you'll find out later."

The moment was broken by a scream coming from the cemetery.

4

Dani ran toward the scream, Reece right behind her. It had sounded like Abbi, and it wasn't a scream of pleasure.

She raced around a mesquite bush to find Abbi in nothing but her bra, hands over her mouth, staring across the fence at a dead goat. Carlos was there too, pantsless, shaking his head. Dani went to her sister and wrapped her in a hug.

"Are you alright?"

Abbi shook her head.

"What happened?" Reece asked, catching his breath and looking around. When he saw Abbi half-naked, he blushed and shifted his gaze to Carlos, then the sky.

Abbi pointed across the fence to where a dark figure lay in a pile on the ground. "I was holding onto the fence, and it just burst through the bushes and fell over. I think it's dead."

"What is it?" Reece walked toward the fence for a closer look.

"A goat," Carlos said.

"It just saw you two fucking and dropped dead?" Reece asked.

"Come on," Dani told Abbi, squeezing her hand. "Let's get

your clothes on." She noticed Reece still had his back to them, and couldn't help but smile. Chivalry wasn't dead.

That or he thought a dead goat was more interesting than a half-naked woman.

"We need to go to a pharmacy too," Abbi whispered. "Carlos was so surprised, he didn't have time to pull out."

Dani shook her head. They were stranded deep in Texas's Big Bend, and her sister was worried about getting the morning after pill.

Abbi pulled on her shorts, then her tank top. Dani picked up Carlos's clothes and tossed them over.

"You like what you see?" he asked with a weak grin.

Dani rolled her eyes and walked over to Reece.

"Abbi's decent," she told him.

"What? Oh. Good."

She put her hand on the small of his back. "You're kind of cute when you're embarrassed," she whispered.

He turned red again. "Really?"

A nod. "So what did you find over here?"

He shrugged. "A dead goat. I didn't want to get a closer look until I was sure I wouldn't be alone if another goat showed up."

Dani bit her lip to keep from laughing. That little bit of sarcasm in his voice was cute, gently mocking Carlos. She liked it. "I'm here," she assured him.

"Good." He took a flashlight from his pocket, and carefully climbed across the fence. On the other side, he stepped over to the goat's corpse and knelt next to it, shining his light along the dead animal's body.

"What do you see?" Dani called to him.

"Bite marks," he replied.

"Bite marks?" She leaned over the fence. "Like a coyote or something?"

Reece shook his head, then walked toward her. He climbed

back over the fence. "It almost looked like a snake, but they were too far apart. Just two puncture wounds in the neck."

"Weird," Dani said.

"Spooky," Carlos added. They turned to find him fully clothed, standing with his arm around Abbi's shoulders. "You scared?" he asked Reece.

He shook his head. "More curious than anything. How do you attack an animal without it making a sound? What can kill with just a bite mark?"

"Maybe it was a snake," Abbi said. "Just a really big one."

Reece shook his head. "I could see where other teeth had pressed into the skin. Almost like a human, some kind of vampire, maybe?"

"Vampire?" Carlos asked. "You're making shit up."

Reece shrugged. "I honestly don't know. I've never seen anything like it, so I'm just spitballing ideas to see what makes sense."

"Let's get back to the fire," Carlos said. "No need to stand around in a spooky cemetery while whatever killed that goat is still out there."

"Did you have to say that?" Abbi shivered as Carlos took her hand and led her toward the gate.

Dani slid her hand into Reece's. "You really think it's a vampire?"

He shrugged. "I don't know what to think. I've never seen anything like it, but that's what I thought it looked like."

They rounded the last mesquite bush to find Abbi and Carlos staring at something between them and the fire. It looked like an overgrown dog, except for the spikes running down its back. Three eyes glowed green as they stared at them, and a low growl rumbled in the beast's throat. Fangs poked out of its mouth on either side of its jaw. Though it sat on all fours, its front legs had hands at the end that were almost human. If it stood, it'd probably be six or seven feet tall, Dani estimated.

"What the fuck is that?" Abbi breathed.

"Fucking monster," Carlos added.

"Just a mutated coyote," Reece said, stepping past them and clapping his hands at the beast. "Go on, get out of here! Shoo!"

It stared at Reece for a moment, and Dani thought it was going to attack. But then it turned and disappeared into the brush.

"Is it gonna come back?" Abbi asked as Reece pushed the gate open.

"Probably not," Dani said. "But we might want to stay in the car, just in case."

5

Dani lay with her head in Reece's lap. She felt safe, curled up with him. He was a protector at heart, an awkward, shy knight who'd stand between her and whatever life threw at them. He'd been ready every step of the way on this misadventure. Food, water, and now she was curled up under an emergency blanket he'd packed.

Next to her was the rifle he'd pulled from his pack and assembled when they climbed into the jeep.

"Survival rifle," he told her. "Everything comes apart and fits into the stock. I almost didn't bring it, but if that thing comes back, we'll be glad I did."

Carlos had shaken his head. "All that runty little gun will do is piss it off."

Dani had smiled. "Don't listen to him."

Now, as she snuggled against him, she found herself wanting to kiss him again. It had been fun.

Something poked her head, and she tried to find it with her hand. It was under Reece's jeans, whatever it was.

When she looked up at him, he'd gone red-faced again.

"Sorry," he said. "I wasn't expecting you to try to grab my hard-on."

"Oh," Dani said.

"Maybe y'all need to get a room," Abbi said from the front seat. She didn't turn her head to look at them, staring out into the darkness around them.

"Do you think it's gone?" Carlos asked.

"No, he's still plenty hard." Dani smiled up at Reece, who was still blushing.

"You know what he meant, Dani," Abbi snapped, but Dani could see the hint of a smile on her sister's face. She'd broken the tension, definitely a positive thing.

"I don't think it will bother us again," Reece said. "It's been alone out here for who knows how long. It was probably curious about the fire, then decided to disappear when it realized there were humans around."

"I hope you're right," Abbi said.

Carlos reached over and patted her hand. "The nice thing about nerds is, they usually are. Just close your beautiful eyes and get some sleep. When you wake up, someone will be here to take us home."

Dani shifted in the backseat. "Maybe someone should stay awake, keep an eye out, you know?"

Reece absent-mindedly ran his fingers through her hair. "I didn't plan to sleep."

Dani smiled up at him. "I hope you planned to keep playing with my hair, though."

A nod. "Your wish is my command."

Dani woke to a thumping noise on the jeep's plastic roof..

"What's that?" she whispered.

"Huh? Sorry," Reece replied. "I must have dozed off."

"Shh!" Abbi hissed from the front. "Maybe if we're quiet, it will go away."

Reece felt around Dani, looking for something, his hand finally landing on her breast.

"Whatcha looking for?" she asked as he froze, realizing where his hand was.

"Your hand. I was gonna hold it..."

"You'll have to take it off my tit to do that," she replied, putting her hand on top of his, but not moving it.

The footsteps on the jeep roof moved toward the front.

"Guys, this ain't the time to be feeling each other up," Abbi hissed.

Dani just squeezed Reece's hand, glad she'd decided to wear a bikini top instead of a bra. Not only was it more comfortable, it let her feel the pressure of Reece's fingers against her skin. If the beast got them, at least she'd die feeling wanted.

The thing on the roof jumped, landing on the hood and turning toward them. Reece squeezed Dani's breast, hard. Abbi gasped.

Dani laughed.

It wasn't the beast they'd seen earlier.

It was a fucking goat.

Abbi let out a sigh of relief. Reece quietly chuckled.

A goat was standing on the hood, gazing at them through the windshield.

"I thought it was..." Reece started to say.

That's when it struck.

It came flying out of the brush next to the road, grabbing the goat around the neck and pinning it to the hood.

Carlos woke with a start. "Jesus fucking Christ, what the hell is that?"

Three glowing eyes looked through the windshield at Carlos. Then the thing licked its lip.

"Son of a bitch, I'm getting out of here!"

"Carlos! Wait!" Reece tried to grab him, but he'd flung the door open and was sprinting away from the jeep.

The beast looked down at the goat, then after Carlos. A grin came to its lips, revealing its pointed canines. Then it jumped off the hood of the jeep and sprinted into the brush after Carlos.

6

Reece climbed into the driver's seat and pulled the door closed as Dani tried to console her sister.

"It's gonna kill him," Abbi sobbed. "Whatever it is, it's gonna kill Carlos!"

"I think it's a Chupacabra," Reece said, staring out the window.

"A what?" Dani asked.

"A Chupacabra," he repeated. "It literally translates to 'goat-sucker.' It's the kind of thing you tell stories about at a Boy Scout campfire." Reece shook his head. "They aren't supposed to be real."

Dani was quiet for a moment. While it was good to know what they were facing, hearing it was some imaginary creature chasing Carlos couldn't be good for Abbi. But they'd all seen it. "Could it be some kind of mutant?" Dani asked. "Like, a coyote or something."

"No." It was Abbi who spoke, surprising both of them. "You saw it. It'd have to swim in a nuclear waste dump to come out like that." She took a deep breath. "So we know what it is. What do we do?"

Reece sighed. "We've got two options. One, we go after it and try to rescue Carlos. Two, we stay here and wait for help."

Dani reached over the seat and squeezed her sister's shoulder. "No matter what we do, we'll do it together."

"Do you really think it'll attack Carlos?" Abbi asked. "You said it's a goat sucker, not a human sucker."

Reece shrugged. "I don't know. This is supposed to be a camp-fire legend..."

"Well, it ain't!" Abbi snapped. "So it's time to grow a pair and face reality!"

Reece jumped back, almost like Abbi had hit him.

"Hey!" Dani cut in. "We're all doing our best here!"

"I know," Abbi said, burying her face in her hands and starting to sob. "It just isn't fair. Carlos is a good guy, a good boyfriend. He doesn't deserve to die at the hands of a chimichanga."

"Chupacabra," Dani and Reece corrected automatically.

"Whatever!" She turned and looked at Dani. "We've got to try to save him. Can we at least try?"

Dani looked at Reece, who nodded. "We can try."

Reece wrapped duct tape around the handle of a long, mean-looking knife, attaching it to a stick they'd found.

"Hurry," Abbi said. "It could have already killed him."

"It'll kill us too if we're not prepared," Reece said calmly, tearing off the tape and examining his work. "Okay." He turned to Dani. "Spear or rifle?"

"Spear," she said, taking the weapon from him. She'd never shot a gun before, but was sure she'd have to hit the Chupacabra to drive it off. It probably wouldn't be best to rely on beginner's luck.

"Alright," Reece said, pulling on his backpack and picking up the rifle. "Stick together."

He led them past the smoldering remains of the fire, and they entered the brush near the cemetery gate. Reece clicked on his flashlight.

"Won't that thing see us coming?" Abbi asked.

"It can probably see in the dark better than we can," Dani said. "This is just evening up the score."

Reece nodded. "There's a good trail, I can see right where they went." He pointed to broken sticks and bent grass with the barrel of the rifle.

They followed the trail as it curved around the cemetery, then climbed a small hill.

"Careful," Reece said. "We're on top of the mine shaft."

The girls nodded. Dani was thankful when the trail descended the other side. How far ahead of them were Carlos and the Chupacabra? Was Carlos alright? Was he dead? Why didn't they hear anything?

The trail led them around to where the shaft entered the mountain, and there, Reece stopped.

"What?" Abbi asked.

He shined his light on a set of footprints.

Sneaker prints headed into the mine.

Paw prints led past it.

Reece put a finger to his lips. Stepping into the entrance of the shaft, he shined the light around, finally settling on a figure sitting behind a large rock.

"Carlos?" he whispered, his voice carrying.

"Reece? Is that you?" came the reply.

"Carlos!" Abbi pushed past Reece and rushed into the shaft. Dropping to her knees, she threw her arms around her boyfriend's neck and kissed him. "You're okay, you're okay, you're okay!"

"Easy baby," he said, smiling. "I got lucky. I tripped coming in here, fucked up my ankle. I thought I was done, but the damn thing went on by."

"Let me see," Reece said, handing Dani the rifle and shrugging out of his backpack. She turned to watch the tunnel entrance, hoping the Chupacabra wouldn't appear.

Behind her, she heard Carlos gasp.

"It's alright," Reece said. "I'm just taking your shoe off so I can see what's going on."

A moment later: "There's some bruising, it's definitely sprained, maybe worse." The light shone past Dani for a moment. "Grab that old shovel over there, we can use the handle to make a splint."

Dani found herself tuning out what was going on behind her with Carlos and focusing on the tunnel's entrance. Would the Chupacabra come back? Or had they succeeded in running it off? She stepped toward the opening, wondering why it had gone past Carlos.

She kicked a small rock, sending it bouncing out the mine entrance into the moonlight.

A dark shape leaped from on top of the shaft, landing on the moving rock as Dani screamed.

7

Dani pulled the trigger until the rifle stopped shooting, the gunfire echoing off the walls of the shaft. She wasn't aiming; she was pointing and hoping for the best.

By the time the sound of the last gunshot faded, there was nothing outside the mineshaft.

"What was that?" Reece yelled, coming to stand next to her.

"I think it was the Chupacabra," she replied, taking a deep breath. The sound of the gunshots in the confined space had made her ears ring, and she shook her head to try to clear them. Reece gently took the gun from her and ejected the clip.

"Did you hit it?" he asked, walking over to his backpack. Pulling out a small cardboard box, he started sliding brass rounds into the clip. When he was done, he put the clip back in the gun and handed it to her.

Dani shrugged. "I didn't see. I'm sorry. One minute, it was there, and I started shooting, then when I stopped, it was gone."

Reece put his hand on hers and squeezed. "It's gone. That's what matters."

Dani looked around. Reece was almost done with the splint on

Carlos's leg. Abbi was snuggled up against Carlos, quietly weeping. Dani wondered if she should be more scared, so her sister wouldn't feel weak comparing herself to Dani.

Fuck that, she thought. *You've been comparing yourself to her for years, she can look up to you for a change!*

Dani turned back to face the entrance. She wondered if she had managed to hit it. Had there been a cry of pain amid the gunfire? Or had that just been her imagination?

She wanted to know.

Dani crept closer to the mouth of the shaft. Staying just inside the entrance, she took out her flashlight and shone it over the ground.

There!

The light reflected off a dark spot on the ground. Dani wasn't sure, but it looked like blood.

She had hit it!

But where was it?

The brush around the opening looked the same, with no sign of the monster. Had it crawled back above the shaft? Or had it taken off, disappearing into the desert?

Baaaaaaaaaaaaaaat!

The sound made her jump, but it definitely came from outside the mine shaft. It was a goat, and it sounded like it was in pain.

Chupacabra!

Of course it would try to feed if it was injured. It would need its strength for whatever it planned to do next. Dani waited, watching the area outside the mine shaft for any sign of movement.

A goat stumbled into the clearing, then collapsed.

Dani didn't need a closer look to know it would have a bite mark in its neck and be drained of blood.

"Everything okay?" Reece asked, wrapping his arms around her waist from behind. Dani wondered why for a moment, then realized: it left her arms free to shoot.

It felt safe, like no matter what monsters were out there, they'd find a way out of this together. It would all be okay. "I think it fed. There's a dead goat out there."

"Okay," he whispered. "I think we're safest in here. When help arrives, they'll find the jeep, and we can signal our position with the gun."

Dani nodded. "Sounds good."

He started to let go of her, but she caught his hand. "Stay with me."

"What?"

"Stay here," she said. "Hold me like you were."

He put his arms around her again, pulling her tight against his body. "I wish I could kiss you."

Dani smiled. "It's probably not a good idea for us to be distracted like that."

He kissed the back of her neck, sending a chill down her spine. "I like that," she said.

"Good," he whispered.

They stayed like that for awhile, Dani holding the rifle, Reece holding her. Occasionally, he'd kiss the back of her neck, and she would smile.

"Do you think it's gone?" she finally asked.

"I think it's waiting," he said.

"Waiting?" She pulled the gun tighter against her shoulder, her eyes scanning the treeline with greater intensity.

"It knows we're in here. It knows we have to come out eventually. It tried taking the offensive, and it didn't go well. So now it's going to wait for us to come out into the open, and hope we let our guard down."

Dani shivered, and Reece squeezed tighter. "Don't worry. I won't let anything happen to you."

8

Blaaaaaaaat!

Dani bolted upright, looking around. Maybe she'd been a little too comfortable in Reece's arms.

"It's trying to draw us out," Reece said, stepping back to give her a better range of motion.

She handed the rifle to him. "Your turn."

As Dani stepped behind him, she checked her watch.

2:17 AM.

Jesus, was daylight that far away?

Another goat wandered into the clearing, then collapsed.

"How can it move like that with no blood?" Reece asked.

"I don't know. Abbi and Carlos said the one they saw did the same thing."

Reece nodded, then chuckled. "Can you imagine if the last thing you saw was two people fucking?"

"You know we can hear you, right?" Carlos asked from behind them.

"I'm just saying," Reece said.

"It is kind of funny, though," Abbi said. "Oh look, humans, what the hell are they doing? *Eggggggt!*" She flopped over into Carlos's lap.

Dani couldn't help but chuckle. Stepping closer to Reece, she put her arms around his waist, just like he'd had his, and rested her head on his shoulders.

"Thank you," she whispered.

"For what?"

"Being you. Making me realize that having a boyfriend might not be so bad."

He froze. "Wait, does that mean...?"

"Do you want it to?"

He nodded.

"Then yeah, it does."

Behind them, someone clapped. "I love a good love story," Carlos called. Dani turned to see Abbi helping him get to his feet. "I've rested long enough. I'll take a turn standing guard."

"You sure?" Reece asked.

He nodded, holding out his hand.

Reece gave him the rifle, then took Dani's hand. "Come on."

They settled a little further in the tunnel than where Carlos had been sitting. Abbi got up to be closer to Carlos, giving Reece and Dani an illusion of privacy.

"You can get some sleep if you want," he said, as they sat down against the tunnel wall.

She snuggled up against him. "Are you sure?"

He shrugged. "I figured you'd be tired. It's been a long night."

"A lot has happened tonight," Dani whispered. "I'm not sure I'm going to be able to sleep."

"I mean, yeah, but if you want to..."

Dani rolled her eyes. He was so clueless. Grabbing his face, she pulled him to her and kissed him, long and slow. He was getting better. They both just needed practice. She felt his hand slide under her tank top, feeling her breast over the bikini top.

"Naughty boy," she whispered, breaking the kiss for a moment.

"Do you want me to stop?"

"Fuck no." She resumed the kiss, and soon his hand slipped under the bikini top.

She'd always wondered what this would be like, all the times she'd seen Abbi making out with her boyfriends, them groping and grabbing each other while they kissed.

Now she knew.

It was more fun than she'd thought possible, falling into someone, exploring each other, feeling and touching things for the first time. Reece was gentle, but also hungry, his fingers finding her nipple and gently pinching.

A moan of pleasure escaped her.

Dani wished she had more to share. Bigger breasts, fuller lips... But it didn't seem to bother Reece.

They broke apart, and even in the darkness, she could see him grinning.

"I think I'm going to have to go to confession," he said.

Dani quietly chuckled. "Altar boy."

"You've made me an altered boy," he whispered, leaning in to kiss her again.

"Carlos! What are you doing?"

Dani's eyes snapped open at the urgency in Reece's voice. She must have drifted off, comfortable and safe in Reece's arms. Now, as her eyes adjusted, she saw a shadowy figure limping toward the mine entrance.

"Carlos!" she snapped.

The figure turned. "What?"

"What are you doing?"

He sighed. "I'm tired of this shit, hiding hurt in a cave waiting to be rescued. What kind of man does that make me?"

"A survivor," Reece said.

"What's going on?" Abbi asked groggily.

"I'm gonna go deal with that Chupacabra," Carlos announced. "I'm gonna tear it limb from limb, then we can all go back to the jeep and sleep and wait for help to arrive without some freak beast attacking us."

Abbi jumped to her feet. "Carlos! No!"

He shook his head. "I've got to, Abbi. Don't worry, I'll be alright." He leaned the gun against the wall, picked up the makeshift spear, then stepped out into the clearing.

"Hey, Chimichanga!" he yelled. "Come out and let's settle this!"

Reece moved toward the rifle. As he reached it, something jumped down from on top of the mine shaft. It landed on Carlos's back, knocking him to the ground.

Abbi screamed. Dani grabbed her, holding her back to keep her from trying to help Carlos as he rolled in the dirt with the Chupacabra.

Reece had the gun up. "I don't have a shot, I don't have a shot, I'll hit Carlos," he muttered.

The Chupacabra pulled Carlos to his feet, a long arm wrapped around his neck. It growled at Reece, standing at the mouth of the shaft, then sank its teeth into Carlos's neck.

"Oh my God," Abbi screamed, trying to pull away from Dani.

"I don't have a shot," Reece repeated, never taking the rifle off the beast.

The Chupacabra let go of Carlos, and he staggered toward the mine shaft. One step. Two steps. Then he collapsed to the ground.

By then, the Chupacabra was disappearing into the brush.

Reece fired after it, emptying the magazine, but there was no sign he'd hit it. He stepped out of the entrance and knelt next to Carlos, putting his fingers to his wrist, then shaking his head.

He stepped back into the cave and sighed. "He's dead."

9

Dani sat with her arms around her sister. What do you say to someone who'd just seen her boyfriend's blood sucked out by a monster that shouldn't exist? "There, there" and "It's going to be alright" didn't seem sufficient.

Reece stood at the mouth of the tunnel, staring out at Carlos's body. Dani wanted to be there for him too, she knew he'd tried to stop Carlos and looked for a chance to take down the Chupacabra and save him. But did her sister need her more?

She couldn't tell.

She wanted to tell Reece to come sit down next to her, to have a chance to console both of them. But someone needed to keep an eye out for the Chupacabra.

So she sat, arms around her sister, wondering what kind of hell she was going through. Just hours earlier, Abbi had been worried about getting the morning after pill. That seemed like an eternity ago after the night they'd had.

She checked her watch. 3:58. The night was crawling by far too slowly. Dani wanted the sun to rise. Somehow, she had a

35

feeling the Chupacabra was nocturnal, and even if it wasn't, the dark made it seem even scarier.

Once the sun came up, the time for nightmares was over.

Deeper in the mine, something growled.

She looked down the shaft into the darkness. Was she hearing things? They were at the entrance, how could anything be deeper in the mine?

Another growl.

Reece turned toward her. "Did you hear that?"

She nodded. Pulling out her flashlight, she aimed it deeper into the shaft.

Three eyes reflected in the dark.

"Son of a bitch!" she yelled, scrambling to her feet.

"Duck!" Reece yelled, raising the rifle.

She dropped, hearing the reports as bullets flew overhead. Something snarled, and Dani turned to look down the shaft.

The eyes were gone.

A howl of pain echoed up the tunnel. Reece grabbed his backpack as Dani pulled Abbi to her feet and picked up the spear.

"Come on!"

They stumbled out into the night. Reece let Abbi and Dani get ahead of him, keeping the rifle aimed at the entrance.

"Where are we going?" Dani asked.

"Back to the jeep!" Reece called.

They raced around the cemetery to the road, then froze.

The jeep's top had been pulled apart, plastic pieces strewn all around it. The seats had been ripped to shreds, with stuffing and fabric scattered everywhere. Only the roof supports and seat frames were still in place, and Dani could see that even they were bent in places.

Abbi sat down in the middle of the road.

"It's hopeless," she whimpered.

"Abbi, come on," Dani said, grabbing her sister's arm and trying to pull her to her feet.

"No! Leave me alone!"

"No!" Dani pulled again. "Damn it, Abbi, you're my sister!"

She snorted. "Like you ever cared about me. I heard all the things you said growing up. 'Abbi the slut,' 'the whore of Abbilon,' that I was going to get some sort of disease." Abbi was sobbing now. "I just wanted to be the cool big sister that you could talk about boys or makeup or life or whatever with, and it felt like you weren't interested!"

Dani sighed, and knelt next to her sister. "Abbi, I'm sorry. I wasn't interested in boys or makeup, or any of the things you were. It's just not who I am. And you trying to force it on me didn't help."

She sniffed. "You were the smart one, Dani. Everyone respected you. Our parents, the teachers, it was always how great Dani is going to be. Meanwhile, everyone looked at me and saw tits and ass."

Dani looked around. Reece was standing nearby, rifle raised, scanning the brush. She looked back down at Abbi.

"Sis, we've got a lot to talk about, but we can't do it if you're dead. Let's get through tonight. Can you do that for me?"

Abbi paused, and Dani held her breath. Then her sister nodded, and together, they got to their feet.

A growl came from the direction of the cemetery.

"Will that damn thing not die?" Dani yelled, turning and raising her spear.

The Chupacabra crawled out of the brush, three eyes moving from Dani to Reece to Abbi. It was stalking, looking for a weakness, wanting to finish the fight as badly as they did.

Reece fired.

The shot hit the Chupacabra in the shoulder. It jumped back, using its other hand to cradle the injury. The spines on its back raised as it let out a low growl, locking its eyes on Reece.

Dani saw her chance.

Spear in hand, she sprinted toward the beast.

10

Dani heard Abbi yelling behind her, but she didn't care.

The Chupacabra turned toward Dani at the last moment, and the knife pierced one of its eyes.

It leapt backward, yowling in pain. Dani had to hold on tight to keep from having the spear yanked out of her hands. Blood dripped from the wounded eye as the Chupacabra stared at Dani. She thrust the spear toward it.

"Go on! Git!" she yelled.

It took a step back, then another.

A gunshot rang out. Another eye blasted open, scattering blood across the ground. With a screech of pain, the Chupacabra turned and disappeared into the brush.

Dani lowered the spear and let out her breath.

The next thing she knew, she was wrapped in a hug.

"Dani, how dare you?" She heard Abbi's voice. "I thought you were gonna get killed, I thought I was going to have to tell Mom and Dad." A pause. "Don't do that to me again!"

"Fine, just don't smother me," Dani mumbled, and Abbi let go.

"What the hell got into you?" Reece asked, coming over.

"I'm tired, I'm hungry, and I've spent the night being stalked by a creature that shouldn't exist." She grinned. "I just needed a little stress relief."

Reece chuckled. "That's my girl." Then he froze for a moment. "Can I say that?"

Dani nodded. "You can say that all you want."

She noticed Abbi shrink a little, and went to put her arm around her. "I'm sorry, Abbi."

Abbi looked up and forced a smile. "It's okay. I know you're not trying to hurt me, I just...Why did Carlos have to be so fucking stupid?"

Dani wrapped her sister in a hug as she broke into tears.

"What now?" Abbi asked when they finally separated.

Reece had gone over to look at the bloody ground where the Chupacabra had been standing. "It's tired, it's hurt. I say we run it down and finish it."

Dani nodded. "We have the advantage. Let's take the fight to it."

"Okay," Abbi nodded. "For Carlos. Let's get it."

Drops of blood reflected off the flashlight beam, giving them an easy path to follow through the brush. They went past the cemetery, past the mine entrance, then along the elevation where the shaft came out of the ground.

"Where do you think it's going?" Dani asked, scanning the desert around them before checking her watch. 4:39 AM. Dawn would be here soon. Looking up, she almost thought there was a faint glow on the eastern horizon.

"I don't know," Reece said. "Maybe it has a nest or a den somewhere."

"What if there's more than one?" Abbi asked.

They froze. Looked at each other in the darkness. Reece was the first to speak.

"I think if there was more than one, they'd hunt in packs. Like dogs. Since we only ever see one, I think it's safe to assume it's alone."

Dani nodded agreement. "That sounds about right."

They followed the trail off the rise and into denser shrub. Reece was moving quickly, almost making Dani wonder if they were walking into a trap.

Baaaaaaaaaaaat!

It came from behind a small rise ahead of them. Reece quickly climbed it, and once on top, raised the rifle and fired. Dani heard a yelp, then thrashing as she ran to join Reece.

She was just in time to see the Chupacabra's tail disappear into the brush.

Beneath them, a goat staggered, unsteady, but alive.

"What happened?" Abbi asked, joining them.

Reece pointed at the goat. "The Chupacabra was trying to feed, but I interrupted it."

"Is it okay?" Abbi asked.

Reece shrugged. "It lost some blood, but it hasn't keeled over yet."

"We should probably kill it," Dani said.

"What?" Abbi asked, wide-eyed.

"There's no telling what being bitten by that thing does, because it's killed all the victims until now. What if a half-bite creates another thing just like it?"

Baaaaaaaaaaaaaaaaaaat! The goat was rolling around on the ground now. *Baaaaaaaaaaaaaaaaaat!*

Reece raised the rifle and fired twice. The goat went still, dark blood flowing from the wounds onto its white fur.

"How are you on bullets?" Dani asked.

"Rounds," Reece corrected with a smile. "I've got about twenty left."

"Will that be enough?" Abbi asked.

He shrugged. "The box had fifty when we started. I hope it's close to dead. I think it has to be. But I can't say for sure."

Dani took a deep breath. "Should we go back to the car and wait for help?"

Abbi looked back the way they'd come for a moment. Then she shook her head. "No. We've come this far. I want to finish this motherfucker."

11

The trail was bloodier now.

"I guess I hit something important," Reece said.

"Not important enough," Abbi said.

Dani took a deep breath. Her sister was grieving, but she still wanted to jump to Reece's defense.

She was surprised to find she missed Carlos. Not his annoying macho bullshit, but the way he was there for Abbi to lean on. With him dead, that weight was falling to her, and she couldn't seek Reece's support without being afraid it would make Abbi feel alone.

Reece turned and winked at her. He was cute. She was surprised she'd fallen for him as fast as she had, though fighting the Chupacabra had done a lot to bring them together.

Want to fall in love with someone? Take them to fight a monster!

They topped another rise, and Reece stopped.

"There," he pointed.

Another shaft jutted out of the ground, and Dani looked just in time to see the Chupacabra disappear inside.

"You think that's how it got behind us earlier?" Dani asked.

Reece nodded.

Next to the opening was a weathered wooden building, the door hanging open and the roof caved in.

"What's that?" Abbi asked.

"Probably where they stored explosives," Reece said.

"Seriously?" Abbi asked.

He shrugged. "I mean, I'm no expert on old mines, but it looks like where you'd keep that kind of stuff."

"So should we go in after it?" Abbi asked. "What if it comes out the other entrance and we just chase it in circles."

"Let's cross that bridge when we get to it," Dani said. "By the time we go in and come out, it'll be almost dawn. Maybe we'll see something in the daylight that we missed in the dark."

Reece nodded. "I'm hoping it just wants to curl up somewhere dark and die. We've done a number on it."

They walked down to the entrance. Dani felt lighter, like the fear was gone. They had the Chupacabra on the run. It wasn't hunting them anymore.

They were hunting it.

It was on its last legs. They would go into the mine, finish it off, then wait for someone to rescue them.

Then they'd head back to campus, and she'd take Reece back to her place and do normal relationship stuff. Snuggle in and watch a movie. Kiss him. Blow him. Fuck him. Make him feel like the Superman he was.

Meanwhile, Abbi would be in mourning.

Shit.

She doesn't need you, a voice said.

You're her goddamn sister, of course she needs you!

Dani looked from Abbi to Reece and sighed. As much as she wanted to just go back to campus and have Reece tend to her needs, she also needed to be there for Abbi.

She shook her head to clear it. *Don't get ahead of yourself, you've got to kill the fucking thing first!*

Reece shined his light down the shaft. It was narrower than the other one, maybe four feet wide. Enough that a man could carry a box or crate through, but that was about it.

"I'll go first," Reece said. "Abbi next, then Dani. Keep an eye behind us. I don't think it's fast enough to get around behind us, especially in the condition it's in, but I don't want to assume."

Dani nodded, gripping the spear tighter and noticing the traces of the Chupacabra's blood on the knife. She might ask Reece if she could keep it after this was over, as a trophy.

Maybe they could use it to cut their wedding cake.

Stop! You've gotta kill the fucking thing first!

A few steps down the tunnel, Abbi grabbed a rusty metal pry bar.

"Now I've got a weapon too," she said.

Dani smiled. "You gonna give it tetanus?"

Abbi grinned back. "Whatever works."

The narrow shaft descended steeply, unlike the tunnel they'd been in before. Every few steps, Dani turned and looked back up the tunnel.

Nothing.

"We're almost to the main shaft," Reece whispered.

A few moments later, they stepped out into the wider tunnel. Reece shined his light on the tunnel floor. "Looks like the blood trail leads deeper into the mine."

"Should we keep going?" Dani asked. "We could just cave in the tunnel and trap it down here."

Reece shook his head. "We could end up trapped in here with it, or worse. If there's one thing I don't want to fuck with, it's several tons of rock and dirt."

Dani reached out and squeezed his hand. "I know something I want to fuck with."

He blushed, making her smile.

Abbi took a step beyond them, deeper into the tunnel. "How far do you think it goes?"

Fur-covered hands reached out of the darkness and grabbed her.

Abbi and Dani screamed.

12

U p close, the Chupacabra looked weak. Two eyes were blown out, and blood was dripping from a wound on its leg. Dani didn't know how it was still standing, much less able to hold on to her sister.

"Let go! Let go! Get off of me!" Abbi tried to elbow and kick it, desperate to get loose.

Reece had the rifle up, but was shaking his head. "I don't have a shot," he said.

Abbi dropped the metal bar with a clang, twisting in the beast's arms as it began to drag her deeper into the mine.

"Dani, help!"

She started forward, and Reece reached out to grab her. "What if it's a trap?" he asked.

"That's my sister!" She twisted loose.

Reece shook his head, but moved deeper into the tunnel. Dani walked next to him, spear raised, keeping her light on Abbi and the Chupacabra. Reece moved his from side to side, making sure there were no surprises waiting for them.

The beast growled at them.

"Dani! Help!" Abbi called, still trying to squirm free.

Dani had a spear. Surely there was less risk of seriously injuring Abbi with it than the rifle, if she accidentally hit her sister. As good as Reece was at first aid, Abbi would probably survive anything short of a beheading.

"Dani! Please."

She darted forward as the Chupacabra sank its teeth into Abbi's neck. Stabbing with the spear, Dani aimed for any exposed flesh, but the creature held on to Abbi.

Strong hands grabbed her and pulled her back.

"Look," Reece said.

The eyes they'd destroyed were reforming, healing themselves as the Chupacabra consumed Abbi's blood. Looking down, Dani saw the wound in its leg was gone too.

Fuck.

"Run!" Reece ordered.

"But Abbi..."

"It's too late, we can't save her," Reece said. Dani glanced at her sister and saw he was right. Her head hung limp, her body pale from the loss of blood.

"Run!" he said, grabbing her hand.

They sprinted up the shaft, tears rolling down Dani's cheeks. Her sister was dead, and if she hadn't been distracted, teasing Reece, she might have stopped the attack, might have saved her.

Reece scooped something off the ground, then stopped and turned around.

The pry bar.

Reaching up, he wedged it into the space above one of the roof beams.

"Keep running," he told her.

"What?"

"We don't have much time. I'm going to trap it."

"No!" She grabbed his arm. "I can't lose you too."

A growl came from further down the tunnel.

It was coming.

"Go, Dani, I'll be right behind you." He smiled at her. "This has been the best night of my life. I love you."

Another growl, this one louder.

"I love you too." She leaned in and kissed him, then sprinted up the tunnel.

Behind her, she heard a creaking sound, then a loud crash. Beneath her, the ground shook. Dani skidded to a stop.

"Reece!"

No answer.

She should go. She should run and get out of here and wait for him outside.

But she had to know. Had to be sure he wasn't hurt. If she could have saved him and she didn't, after what had happened with Abbi, she'd never forgive herself.

Dani moved slowly down the tunnel, shining the flashlight around. Some of the supports looked like they were struggling to hold the redistributed weight of the tunnel's roof. This was dangerous, and she knew she should go, but she had to know.

There!

She saw Reece's head sticking out of a mound of rubble, a peaceful look on his face. As she got closer, she saw his body had been crushed by a massive rock.

But his face looked peaceful, reflecting the spirit of the man she'd spent the last few hours falling for.

This was wrong, so fucking wrong! She'd never get to hug him again, never hear his voice, never make him blush, never feel his hands on her body.

She fell to her knees, gently reaching out to caress his face.

"I love you, Reece," she whispered through tears. "I'm sorry."

Above her, one of the beams creaked. For a moment, she

thought about staying here, being buried forever with Reece and Abbi.

But then would they have died in vain?

She had to go, had to get out of here.

Then she saw something shining against Reece's skin.

Quickly, she took off his necklace and put it in her pocket. Leaning in, she kissed his lips one last time before turning and heading up the mine shaft.

13

Dani staggered out of the portal. Above her, the sky was lit up in orange, pink, and purple as the first part of the sun crept over the horizon.

She was alone.

They were all gone.

Carlos.

Abbi.

Reece.

She wanted to cry, but no tears would come. She was all cried out.

She took the necklace out of her pocket and put it on. It felt better. Almost like Reece was still there, hugging her.

He'd said this had been the best night of his life. In some ways, it'd been the best night of hers.

In others, it'd been hell.

The Chupacabra was done, dead under the cave-in, or maybe trapped behind it. If it had survived, she wondered how long it would take to starve, to wither away in the darkness with no hope of rescue.

Dani wanted it to suffer for everything it had put her through.

She walked around the cemetery, spear still in her hand. The rifle was gone, buried with Reece. If she had to defend herself, she hoped the spear would be enough.

She got to the spot where the fire had been and stopped.

A white pickup truck with green stripes was parked behind the jeep.

Border Patrol.

Two green-uniformed agents, a male and a female, got out and walked toward her.

"Are...are you okay, ma'am?" the woman asked. She was older, gray hair pulled back in a ponytail under her cap.

Dani nodded, then looked down. Her clothes were bloody, dirty, and torn, the skin on her arms and legs scratched and bruised. She looked like she'd been through hell. "I'm fine."

How was she going to explain it? The Chupacabra, the deaths, everything she'd been through? She'd survived it, but having to explain it felt like an even greater burden.

"We got a call about some kids who came out exploring and never made it back," the man said. Young, Hispanic, definitely a guy who thought he was cool because of his job. Any other time, she'd think he was handsome, but now, he was just another pile of flesh.

"It's been a long night," Dani said.

"Looks like it," the man replied, nodding toward the destroyed jeep. "Did you have alcohol? Drugs? Something to take you on a trip?"

"What? No, never!"

"Where are your friends?" the woman asked.

"It killed them," Dani said.

"It?" the man asked.

"The Chupacabra."

"Chupacabra?" The female agent looked at the man. "What the hell's a Chupacabra?"

"A mythical creature," he replied before turning back to Dani. "Are you sure you haven't taken any psychedelic drugs? Maybe someone slipped them to you without you realizing?"

"I'm not on drugs!" Dani snapped. She'd never even smoked weed, now these assholes thought she just dreamed up the hell she'd endured.

"Ma'am," the man said. "There's no such thing as..."

His eyes went wide, and his hand dropped to his gun. Dani saw the woman doing the same thing, and knew what it meant.

The damn thing was behind her.

She dropped to the ground, looking up to see the hairy, human-like hands grabbing the air where she'd been a moment before.

"Why won't you die?" she screamed, taking the spear and ramming it into the beast's chest, going behind the ribcage to where its heart should be.

Did the damn thing even have a heart?

Dani heard gunshots as the agents opened fire. One of the monster's eyes blew out, then another. It staggered backward, then fell forward across Dani, pinning her down.

"Jesus! Fuck!" she heard the male agent yell.

The monster's remaining eye looked at Dani for a moment, then closed for the last time.

The Chupacabra was dead.

The agents rushed forward, struggling to lift the monster off her so she could get free. Dani managed to squirm out, then got to her feet. They stood together, looking down at the Chupacabra's body.

"So," Dani finally managed to say. "Still think I'm on drugs?"

ACKNOWLEDGMENTS

This story would not have been possible without the help of a number of people, to whom I am sincerely thankful.

Chloe York for her editing expertise and creative ideas.

Cyan for being Cyan.

Rebecca for being Rebecca.

Wednesday for her attempts at editing assistance and technical support.

Atlas for the distractions.

Anna for her love and support.

And you, the reader, for picking up this book and reading this far.

Thank you.

ABOUT THE AUTHOR

D.L. Winchester lives in the foothills of southern Appalachia. A former mortician, his work searches the darkness to find tales worth telling. He is the author of over three hundred obituaries, numerous short stories, the story collection Shadows of Appalachia, and the flash fiction collection A Terrible Place.

In his spare time, he can be found searching for inspiration in the world around him and trying to keep his children from becoming the next generation of horror villains.

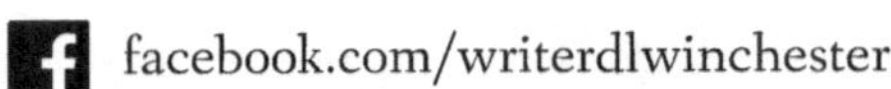 facebook.com/writerdlwinchester

If you are a fan of horror stories and tales, you'll want to follow Undertaker Books.
We're bringing you stories to take to your grave.